COFFEE!!!

Stories of Extreme Caffeination

COFFEE!!!

Stories of Extreme Caffeination

Bob Biderman

BLACK
APOLLO
PRESS

First published by Black Apollo Press
Cambridge, England
© Bob Biderman, 2016
PB: ISBN; :9781900355643
HB: ISBN: 9781900355889

Cover Image: Kevin Biderman
Drawing on Page 6: Cat Webb

For a full catalogue of Black Apollo titles, please visit our website: www.blackapollopress.com

Other Books by Bob Biderman

Technofarm

A People's History of Coffee and Cafes

The Strange Case of Israel Lipski

A Knight at Sea (as R.J. Raskin)

Sacha Dumont's Amsterdam

Strange Inheritance

Genesis Files

Judgement of Death

Paper Cuts

Mayan Strawberries

Letters to Nanette

Red Dreams

Moishe Kaplan and the SDS Murders

Anna and the Jewel Thieves (with David Kelley)

The Polka-Dotted Postman (with Cat Webb)

Further Education

Romancing Paris. Again.

Left-Handed Portuguese Zen

I

He opened the cupboard and stared in disbelief at the emptiness within. There wasn't any coffee left. He had forgotten to stop at the Algerian on his way back to his room and had used every bean in the barren tin that sat topless, open and forlorn, on the most reachable shelf above. Yesterday, when he had thought about replenishing his stock, he considered purchasing a packet of Kopi Luwak – Sumatran civet coffee. It was similar to the Vietnamese Ca Phe Chon – better known as 'weasel coffee' – except the Sumatran civet (a cat-like animal that looks something like a mongoose) shits the beans out whereas the Vietnamese weasel regurgitates them, so the berries of these two prized varieties stew a while in either weasel puke or civet crap before being collected by luckless peasants whose job it is to bag those pungent droppings. Connoisseurs (namely Daisy – a coffee snob if there ever was one) thought it superb (the roasted coffee, that is – not the trip through civet gut) but at £22 for 57 grams it was a high price for a fix, he told her (even though only 500 kilos of the stuff was produced each year for the entire world market – whatever kinky market that was). Coke was cheaper (snort versus sip) and more efficient if it were speed she was after, he said. But it didn't linger on the palate, she replied. The civet stuff had an aura of the wild. And with that he couldn't argue.

That was then. Now, this bloody, headachy morning, he peered into the void and sighed (or moaned). He would have bellowed but the walls were thin and it was 6 AM and nothing – repeat, nothing! – was open between his place on Gower Street and Smithfield Market on the other side of town (at least nothing he knew of and he had sniffed out the best and the worst of the coffee dives for miles around).

How could he have forgotten? After all, there was a note writ boldly in red – BUY COFFEE!!! – adhered to the door of the fridge. But the fridge did not accompany him on his way back from the British Library. There was just room enough on his bicycle for himself, his computer and a small bag of COFFEE!!! had he been more focused on his bodily needs (or what they would be at 6 AM).

And then he spotted it way back on the shelf above, hidden in the shadows like a sad, forgotten friend, waiting to be recognised with nothing more than half a smile or a terse hello but knowing down deep that it will forever be ignored. He reached up and brought it down. For the life of him, he couldn't even remember taking it when he had moved house some years ago. But then he recalled Daisy, in the rather mock-horrified tone she used when trying to sound outraged but was actually fascinated at someone's supposed gaucheness (snob that she was), asking him what the hell was in that silly-looking bottle (even though she knew perfectly well) and what it was doing there polluting the shelves. It wasn't her kitchen he mistakenly reminded her. 'Mistakenly' not because it actually was her kitchen but because saying that just emphasised the boundaries he'd imposed on their relationship which simply made her pout and then respond in an even more prissy manner as punishment for him having rubbed it in.

He brought it down and set it on the counter and stared at it as if to ask what it was doing there – to whomever would respond (either him or the bottle, itself, as there was no one else around at the moment). The shape was similar to a bottle of HP sauce and the colour was similar as well (if the sauce had properly matured in the back of a cabinet for twenty odd years).

The label read 'Camp'. There was more on the label but it was that word, 'Camp', scripted across the side in an easy shade of blue with the 'C' elongated eastwards till it met the tail of the 'P' in a rather charming act of copulation, as if to say that the image underneath of a kilted Scotsman having a pleasant drink with a smiling Sikh outside a military tent flying a red pennant on which was written 'Ready. Aye, ready!' was all part of a unifying theme of peace, brotherhood and love (the metaphor, of course, could be taken in a number of ways, giving 'Camp' an extra fillip in places like Soho). But this particular bottle also connected him to a string of sensations from his childhood – a taste, a fragrance, a texture, a song, a poem and a story.

Solomon Bundy. That was his name – like it or not. He didn't. His friends called him 'Sol'. Daisy called him 'Solly'. She was the only one who could get away with it.

His father was a military man – by default. Called up for service in World War II, he remained for lack of anything else and rose up the ranks to a middling position because that's what happened to young men like him who kept their nose clean and minded their 'Ps' and 'Qs'. He had no real interest in an army career. He was merely a civil servant

– in military uniform. For all the years he lived at home, there was only one military man Solomon Bundy heard his father speak of fondly. And that was Major General Sir Hector Macdonald, otherwise known as 'Fighting Mac – the scourge of Afghans, Boers and the Dervishes of Sudan'.

Major General Sir Hector Macdonald was known to have been the model for the original label created for Camp Coffee back in 1890 when Mr. Paterson (not yet a family man), first brought it out at his factory in Glasgow. Back then the label wasn't quite as friendly and communal as the one Solomon had at hand. The 1890 version showed Sir Hector (the hero of Sudan) sitting in a chair at a small table outside his encampment with two lesser ranking men seated on the ground. Behind him, a black servant is carrying a tray with a bottle of Camp Coffee clearly on show. When he was young, Solomon used to gaze at that label and imagine himself there listening to Sir Hector as 'the scourge of Afghans, Boers and Dervishes' regaled them with stories of his heroic adventures. But the more he stared, the more his focus seemed to shift toward the black servant bringing a bottle of Camp to the officers – similar to the bottle Solomon was holding. And he would try to make out the label on the picture of the bottle being carried on the tray, imagining that it was exactly the same as what was on his bottle, only smaller. And the label on that label was even tinier than that. And the label on the label on the label …. his mind boggled. How far did it go back? Forever, he supposed. (That notion, he recalled, was his first brush with the idea of an infinite universe. So even at an early age, coffee was already to blame for its mind altering powers, if only by proxy.)

But the story of Sir Hector didn't end there. It was for something else that his father would sometimes (after a night of heavy drinking) hold the bottle of Camp out afore him and recite in a deep, throaty baritone, the truly awful poem by Robert W. Service: 'A Life Tragedy'. And staring at that ghastly label, faded and starting to peel, the words came back to him like a compulsive advertising jingle one tries so hard to forget only to hear it over and over again in one's head in the most unhappy form of self-inflicted torture:

A pistol shot rings round and round the world;
In pitiful defeat a warrior lies.
A last defiance to dark Death is hurled,
A last wild challenge shocks the sunlit skies.
Alone he falls, with wide, wan, woeful eyes:
Eyes that could smile at death—could not face shame
Alone, alone he paced his narrow room,
In the bright sunshine of that Paris day;
Saw in his thought the awful hand of doom;
Saw in his dream his glory pass away;
Tried in his heart, his weary heart, to pray:
"O God! Who made me, give me strength to face
The spectre of this bitter, black disgrace."

Sir Hector had risen from the lower

classes, just as Solomon's father. But unlike Solomon's dad (who simply died of boredom), Sir Hector met a bitter, black, disgraceful end, having been accused (wrongly many say) of love that dared not speak its name (at least back then – nowadays, Solomon thought, he would have shouted it to the heavens and then been given the Silver Cross). The bitter end, however, came from a bullet in the brain when Sir Hector aimed his pistol at his very own head and pulled the trigger with his very own hand.

After that bit of knowledge, Camp Coffee never quite tasted the same.

II

The phone rang just as he was spooning several heaping glugs of Camp into a big brown cup embossed with the picture of a clock grinning madly with wild eyes, its multiple hands pointing to the numbers 6, 8, 10, 12, 2 and 4. Underneath its maniacal leer, in letters of bold maroon was written, shakily (as if drawn by someone with severe astigmatism) the words, 'COFFEE TIME!'

Looking in the direction of the incessant ringing, he was aware that his reflexes had been short-circuited by caffeine deprivation and he was left in a state of immobility, not knowing whether to pour the water from the insistent kettle which had finally come to a gurgling boil into his crazed cup or to answer the infernal phone, each ring of which had become like a jackhammer pounding into his skull. Decisions like that defy logic. It is not one for pencil pushers or even the smug sophistication of a computer. It's more like the reaction of a mad dog when beset on one side by a smirking cat and on the other by a meaty bone. Does the canine ponder his options or simply react? And when he reacts, which way does he go?

Solomon being a man, and more intelligent (supposedly) than a dog, mad or not, went both ways at once, grabbing the phone with one hand and the boiling kettle with the other, splashing the hot water on himself as he frantically poured and shouting, 'Ow! Ow! Ow! God damn fucking shit!' into the receiver.

There was a deep, dark silence on the other end. Like the echoing nothingness one might encounter in an endless hole situated at the most distant, far off corner of the universe.

'Hello?' he repeated, with a bit more humility while under his breath he uttered one more 'shit!' very quietly as he felt his hand throb in pain because of its recent scalding.

'You haven't had your coffee yet, have you?' It was Daisy. Her voice was chastising.

'I'll call you back in a minute,' he said, ditching the phone. And running to the sink, he turned on the tap and stuck his wounded hand underneath the cooling waters.

The phone rang again with even more insistence than before. He let it ring (in the way a battered beast might respond to Pavlov's bell when finally realising, after years of abuse, that the whole thing was a set-up) and poured some water from the cooling kettle into the maniacal cup, stirring the brownish goo frantically until it dispersed its essence of chicory, sugar and coffee flavouring into the now muddy fluid before taking a greedy gulp and then, with a gagging noise that would have woken the dead if there were any dead to wake, spat what had regurgitated from his unwilling stomach back through his oesophagus and into the sink.

He remembered why he hated the stuff. And he blamed Napoleon.

Coffee? Napoleon? Waterloo? What are you thinking about now, you caffeine crazed idiot, he said to himself, as he tore through the shelves searching for a stash he might have hidden for days like today.

It was the Continental Blockade, Daisy had informed him – and, unlike most of what Daisy said, it had stuck in his head.

The French had all the pasta they wanted from Italy, all the olives from Greece, the oranges from Spain, all the herring from the Dutch – but the British ruled the waves and they impounded all the coffee from the Americas. What was Napoleon to do? His army might have lived on sour dough bread and liver pate but they marched on caffeine. And their chief source of the bean was coming from their plantations in the Caribbean whose shipments were impounded by the British fleet to Napoleon's dismay and eternal headache.

'The true history of the world is not made from battles and blood,' his father had told him in one of those rare moments of wisdom detached from his dreadfully long association with the military, 'those events are incidental. The real history of change and transition has to do with food and drink and bodily desires. If you want to know why things happened and why they didn't you need to look at the commodities – sugar, salt, oil, bread, wine and coffee. Who had what – and who didn't; that's all you need to know.'

When Napoleon found out he didn't have coffee in the state larder – at least enough to feed his grumpy soldiers – it was then he knew he was in very bad trouble. And that's when he discovered the bloody root. Chicory! Roasted and ground it could increase the supply of coffee rations three or four or even six to one. The troops had their ersatz juice and Napoleon, briefly at least, was able to get them marching again.

Napoleon's chicory business, of course, was simply supposed to be a stopgap measure. But like many atrocious and artificial war-time foods created to replace short supplies of wholesomeness (think of SPAM!), the soldiers had acquired a taste for this treacle-like guck which, in the their sordid nostalgia, became like swillish ambrosia. Thus had chicory remained a convenient additive, even after Napoleon was sent into exile, to the great delight of coffee merchants who were now able to cut their expensive import with cheap home-grown filler (anything brownish or black) similar to the way coke dealers would later cut their product with inert starch, chalk or rat poison (anything white).

The phone rang again. He answered it. 'Sorry,' he apologised. 'I was in a fix...'

'You mean you needed a fix, don't you?' she replied. And without waiting for a response (if there was one in the offing – which, from experience, she doubted as he wasn't as quick on the uptake as she was), she continued, 'I've got you some translation work. Don't bother thanking me, just be at the Monmouth. 9 AM – on the dot...'

'Whoa. Slow down, Daisy. What's this about?'

'Got to rush…'

'Who am I meeting?'

'The Egyptian…'

'The Egyptian?'

'Yes, you won't have any trouble recognising him. He always wears a fez.'

'If he's Egyptian, he'll be wearing a tarboosh…'

'What?'

'A tarboosh. Comes from the Persian – 'sar 'meaning head and 'poosh' meaning cover. It's almost the same – brimless, made of felt. But the tarboosh is cone-shaped. The fez is more rounded…'

'OK. I get the picture…'

'It's worn in Turkey…'

'The tarboosh?'

'No. The fez. The tarboosh is worn in Egypt…'

'I always called them 'fez' – all those cylindrical red hats topped with a tassel. Cute…'

'It's a tarboosh in Egypt. The fez was worn in Turkey. Until Atiturk banned them...'

'Why did he ban them? They're cute...'

'Because the Ottomans wore them and Atiturk was against everything the Ottomans were for...'

'Including the tarboosh?'

'Including the fez. There was something called the 'Hat Law' enacted in the mid 1920s...'

'Outlawing the fez?'

'Yeah. In the early 19th century Sultan Mahmud Khan II was keen on modernizing what was left of the Ottoman empire so he tried to get everyone to adopt European dress...'

'By wearing a fez?'

'By wearing suits instead of robes – but hats were trickier...'

'Why was that?'

'Because European hats had brims and Moslem men were supposed to prostrate themselves in prayer. So a brimless hat seemed better than a bowler. But then a hundred years later Ataturk went and banned them…'

'Solly!'

'What?'

'I've got to go…'

'Don't you want to know why the fez is so distinctly red?'

'Later. The Monmouth at 9. See the Egyptian with the fez…'

'You mean the tarboosh.'

'Yes, yes, whatever. Just be there!'

Daisy might have sounded abrupt to someone listening in, but she knew her customers. Solomon was an excellent translator (or so he was told) but a very poor businessman – which, for someone who depended on freelance assignments to make ends meet, was problematic. Daisy, however, was brilliant at organising other people's lives. And, as Solomon was terrible at organising his own, she was a perfect match for him – as long as he could keep her out of his kitchen and, in fact, out of his bedsit/office/studio. He preferred staying at her flat for their romantic interludes and then, after a day or two or three, vanishing back into his own inner world. Daisy, of course, resented this shutting out. But Solomon was the first man she ever found in her thirty-six and a half years on earth who was absolutely honest with her and could be both gentle and charming as well as a pain-in-the-neck (as were all men, according to her). What's more they had a nice, easy banter that could go on for hours concerning esoteric subjects that perhaps only seventeen people in the world would find interesting or worth more than a twenty second sound bite that could be switched off in ten. In short, Daisy and Solomon were two people well suited to each other – almost.

It was the 'almost' bit that caused them a certain amount of problems. But all things considered, it was a perfectly decent relationship, even if they did hang up on each other now and then.

III

Once outside, his caffeine craving subsided in the freshness of the air. (Rhetorically speaking, joining 'fresh air' and 'London' in the same sentence – or even paragraph – is what's known as an oxymoron. Being a linguist, however, Solomon knew that in ancient Greek, *oxus* meant 'sharp' and *moros* meant 'foolish', so there was a sense that the etymology of the term was pointing in a different direction from where he was headed as there was nothing pointedly foolish in talking about 'London' and 'fresh air' in the same breath – if one could take a breath long enough outside in the pollution to actually say all that. It wasn't pointedly foolish – just absurd. And absurdity, to him, was a different creature altogether. Nothing foolish about it.)

On the other hand, the idea of 'subsidence' is relative to some sort of starting point. As Solomon's caffeine craving on a scale of 1 to

10 was probably around 53, saying that the craving 'subsided' most likely got it down to 41 – or 36 at the very least. In other words, he still had some way to go before his hands stopped shaking as if he were playing an invisible bongo drum and the thumping in his head would be less like an elephant doing a jig atop his skull and more like a foxtrotting chimpanzee.

Still, he could walk – though his legs were a bit floppy. And since the hour was coming closer to the movement of traffic and people that makes up what we call 'the business day,' chances were good that he would find a place where he could purchase a cup of coffee. He wasn't choosy. By now anything would do as long as it had caffeine. It could come in a cup or in a hypodermic syringe. He'd prefer a cup, but if that wasn't on offer, he'd take the needle.

Then, in the not too distant horizon – in fact just a few hundred paces down Gower Street – he saw it. Were his eyes deceiving him? Was this a mirage? Was it an hallucination thrown before him by his addled brain, too scrambled to think in words but so desperate for a shot of java that it was creating visions like semaphore codes? What was it he saw on the still deserted street? Could it be? And if it was, why hadn't he seen it before?

He approached it like a thirsty man emerging from an arid desert. He half expected it to disappear. And when it didn't, he wondered why. Mirages were supposed to disappear, weren't they? If not, why call it a mirage? What kind of ridiculous mirage was this that refused to go away? If it was so bloody stubborn, it should be called a different name. Like a 'non-mirage' or something of the sort. And then it occurred to him: wait a second! If it's a non-mirage, then it's opposite of a mirage, otherwise why call it 'non-'? And if it's the opposite...

It was at that moment he stuck out his hand and touched the thing that wouldn't go away.

It was a wooden cart of simple construction that had been made into a portable stall. A plaque hanging loosely from a crosswire between two upright posts affixed to either side of the cart had a picture of a cup with trickles of steam rising upward in little curlicues and, underneath, the words, 'Pasqua's Coffeehouse.'

Standing directly underneath the sign was a man, rather small, rather lithe, with eyes that smiled like a crescent moon and seemed to sparkle, catching what little light there was in the gloom of the morning and refracting it through the prism of his gaze into a magnetic radiance.

The little man behind the plank of wood that served as a counter, nodded his head in a friendly way to Solomon who was standing, bemused and still unbelieving, before this curious apparition.

'Shalom!'

Solomon raised an eyebrow.

'You are in luck,' said the man, tugging at the white scarf wrapped loosely around his head, something like a turban. 'Today I have roasted some very special beans that have come to me from Sa'na in the mountains of Yemen...'

IV

There was a rosy hue to the once polluted sky. The birds were singing in the trees and in the streets people danced and frolicked. But it was the colours, he thought – the colours...

He could feel the reds and blues and yellows on the tip of his tongue; like effervescent sweets they exploded in his mouth, filling his head with a multitude of miniature rainbows from the Garden of Earthly Delights that tingled in his nostrils with fragrant murmurs of mountain streams in far off lands where fish and fowl and fury things cavorted in the harmony of a beneficent universe.

What's more, he could focus his eyes.

And for a remarkable moment, he had the strength of a thousand lions. (Small lions, perhaps a bit long in the tooth having been in the circus.)

To say the coffee that Solomon drank at Pasqua's makeshift coffeehouse was 'good', is something of an understatement. It was...

Simply the best? No, that hardly hit the mark. We're on a different scale of measurement, he thought. Can tap water from rusty pipes in a tenement house be compared with the ambrosia imbibed by ancient gods from streams where Diana herself would bathe and Odysseus was once anointed with the liquid essence that gave him back his powers to become a Trojan horse?

He rang Daisy on her mobile. 'Hey! You'll never believe this…'

'That you can string more than three words together without stopping to curse? I guess you've had your coffee fix…'

'Yeah, some coffee…'

'If you like it, remember to get the name of the plantation…'

'It's from Sa'na….'

'In Yemen? Not likely…'

'Why not?'

'They haven't exported from there for over a hundred years…'

'Well, the guy who made it said it was from there….'

'Where'd you have it?'

'At a little makeshift place on Gower Street. Pasqua's…'

She laughed. 'You're having me on, aren't you?'

'No…'

'Listen, I'm in the middle of something right now. Call me later. And remember your meeting at the Monmouth. The Egyptian with the fez…'

'Tarboosh…'

'Whatever…'

He decided not to take his bike. It was a fine day for walking and he felt great. Besides, it was just a short hop to where he was headed: down Gower Street, right on Drummond, left down Foundry Mews, right onto Tolmer's Square, left onto Hampstead Road, straight down Euston Road bearing left onto Tottenham Court Road, walking down Tottenham for a while and then left onto Denmark Street, right onto Flitcroft Street, left onto Stacey Street, left again onto New Compton Street, right onto St.

Giles Passage, straight into Mercer Street and then entering the roundabout that connected him with the tip of the 'V' where Mercer hit Monmouth.

By the time he arrived, the buzz had worn off. London had become dreary again.

V

Seven Dials, where the Monmouth is located, was an area that long had fascinated him. It was the curious nature of the place – a roundabout with seven streets radiating out like spokes of a wheel. And then there was that wonderful pillar, like an ancient artefact – an obelisk or totem or the like – and just below its pointy top, six faces, six clocks (sundials, actually). There should have been seven – for Seven Dials – but the number of radiant streets were originally six, the seventh came later. Each street had the face of a sundial at its terminus – six streets, six dials. Then came the seventh. A street without a dial.

He recalled showing this curious monument to Daisy and then launching off into an exceptionally convoluted and tangential lecture about some obtuse etymology that had a peculiar meaning to him and, because Daisy actually loved him (sort of), also became of interest to her (at least, that's what he allowed himself to believe). For historical interest (simply that − nothing more intended), this is what he told her:

"'Dial" is one of those marvellous words that evolved, through many twists and turns, from the Latin, originally coming from "*dies*" which, itself, meant "day". Our use of the term most likely originated from the Middle English "*rota dialis*" or "daily wheel" which gave us a whole slew of words, including "sundial", rather cleverly combining the concept of circular motion with the idea of passage of time. Over its long and dusty journey, "dial" − a pleasant little word, don't you think? − came to mean "something round" (like a clock face), with a sense of rotation as well, so that when the telephone was eventually discovered (a term I prefer to 'invented' as it has more of the actual gestalt − implying that "telephone" was always there just waiting to be found − you see what I mean? No? Anyway...) the rotary wheel that came with the phone's early evolution, was itself called a "dial" followed by the verb, 'to dial', which meant "to turn the circular mechanical bit with one's finger in order to process a call". And then, when the circular bit morphed into push buttons, the language came with it, like a little obedient dog, so "to dial a number" continued meaning "to make a phone call" even though the sense of the rotating wheel had been lost in the flurry of terrible techno-babble. Are you following me?'

"I'm following you but what's the point?" she said.

"Does everything have to have a point?" he asked, a bit disgruntled.

"Most things do, yes…"

Maybe that was the difference between her and him (or him and her). He didn't believe that things had to have a point at all.

'I wanted to give you some idea of why it's called Seven Dials,' he said, gesturing toward the monument. 'Most people don't know what a "dial" is anymore…'

'But there are only six,' she reminded him.

'What?'

'Dials. There are only six dials. See? One, two, three, four, five, six...' She counted them off on her fingertips. 'So why isn't it called "Six Dials"?'

He scratched his head. "Six Dials doesn't sound as good, does it?"

Then he launched off on another explanation:

'In the early part of the 17th century, the area now known as Seven Dials was marshy fields. But as London was growing by leaps and bounds, it was prime land for developers. And there was this guy named Neale...'

'Yeah,' she said, 'I know. Neale's Yard. Great place for face creams and shampoo that doesn't rust your scalp...'

'Yes, well... history has a strange way of transforming names of people and things into something very far removed from what they were or what they ever hoped to be. That Mr. Neale is known for hair tonic rather than cleaning up a putrid swamp, is more than ironic...'

'Why ironic?'

'Because if he were like most 17th century gentlemen adventurers, he probably washed his hair six times in his life. Don't you find it ironic that nowadays we'd rather build mental statues to people we connect with herbal infusions and body lotions rather than with urban design?'

She shrugged. 'Herbal infusions and body lotions are important too…'

He felt she was probably having him on, but he knew that partly it was just their curious dialectical banter. On the other hand, who in the world would have a conversation like this, at midday, in the middle of the street – madmen aside?

'Look,' he said, 'Seven Dials is a metaphor. Standing here we're only what? A ten minute walk from Leicester Square? But back then it was a smelly swamp at the city's fringe. So what happened? And why? Neale was a visionary but he was also a man of his time. A decade before, Neale probably would have been selling shares in tulips…'

'Tulips?' She looked at him questioningly. 'Tulipmania was in 1634. That was a few years before Neale's time.'

'...or something. Anyway, the Dutch are involved up to their necks. Think about it, here we are in the late 1600s. London is on the move. No longer a sleepy backwater, she's starting her long and determined march into destiny. And it's all because of the Dutch...

'Wait a second. How did the Dutch get into this soliloquy of yours? I thought we were talking about Neale and Seven Dials which was actually Six?'

'The Dutch were involved in everything – you must have figured that out by now. At least they were by the late 1600s. Most people don't know because they were very quiet about it. Not the in-your-face stuff of the French and the Germans. They just went about their business. How many people really know about the Glorious Revolution?'

'It was only "glorious" if you were Protestant,' she reminded him.

'It wasn't about religion. That was just a convenient excuse. Godly loyalties changed depending on the prevailing wind. What's important is that in 1687, England became a centre for international finance – after the Dutch marched in...'

'At the invitation of the Anglican church,' she reminded him. 'Anyway they weren't Dutch...'

'Who?'

'The invading troops were mercenaries. Half of them were Swedes and Scots..'

'Yeah. There were even a few hundred natives brought over to fight from the Americas. But don't forget, a good number of those mercenaries were Catholic. Did you know there were even suggestions a lump of money that went to finance this so-called Protestant invasion came directly from the Pope because he hated Louis of France more than William of Orange?'

'That's just my point. They weren't Dutch.'

'So who were the Dutch? The Portuguese Jews? The refugees from the Spanish

Netherlands? The Swedes, the Swiss, the Poles, the Scots who manned their army and crewed their ships? Holland in 1680 was a hodgepodge. Being Dutch wasn't a thing, it was an idea...'

Her eyes were starting to glaze over. 'I know you don't believe in points, but does this have anything to do with Seven Dials or Six Dials or anything else I might have missed?'

'Like I said, it's the Dutch connection. In 1690 William of Orange granted Thomas Neale, a land developer, some marshland known as 'Cock and Pye Fields'. Ordinarily there would have been a street or two and several rows of houses constructed. But Neale, rather ingeniously (and as a way of maximizing his profit), devised a plan whereby six streets –a seventh came later – would branch out from a central hub on which was built a magnificent pillar – a sundial with six faces, so that each of the radiating streets would be overseen by its own timekeeping apparatus. But that kind of imaginative urban expansion took finance. And William of Orange brought with him capital, fiscal expertise and new methods of servicing debt. What could be more Dutch than that?'

'Is that it?' she asked, rather hopefully.

'There's a coffee connection, you know.'

Her eyes lit up. 'There is? What is it?'

Now that he had her attention, he thought he'd let her dangle. 'You know that engraving I have on my wall?'

'The Hogarth in your kitchen?'

It was Gin Lane, William Hogarth's iconic engraving of London low life in a drunken bacchanal. Central to the eye, in the foreground, a woman sits at the top of a steep flight of stairs. She's dressed in rags, her blouse torn open exposing her saggy nursemaid's bosom. Her body slumps like a beat-up Raggedy Anne. Her face wears a silly dissipated grin. The poor woman is so far gone that she's blissfully unaware her baby has fallen from her arms over the side of the railing and is plunging to its almost certain death. Except it isn't. Instead it's trapped forever in the aspic of the artist's pen, a look of surprised terror embossed on its angelic countenance. The falling baby is frozen in time. As is its drunken mother. As is the grotesquely distorted man behind her gnawing on a monstrous bone while a mangy dog chews at the other end. And to the side another mother is eternally fixed in the act of feeding her child a glass of demon gin.

'How can you have that horrible scene hanging in your kitchen?' she asked him.

'If it was anyone else, it would be horrible and I certainly wouldn't have it in my rooms. But it's Hogarth. And because it's Hogarth, it's not horrible at all. In fact, it's almost charming.'

'Charming?' Hey, maybe there's something about this guy I don't know, she thought.

'Like Bruegel.'

'I don't think I've ever heard "Bruegel" and "charming" used in the same sentence, either,' she said.

'So you heard it from me first…'

'As with many things,' she admitted.

'Charming', of course, wasn't the word for Hogarth's Gin Lane. And both he and she knew that the term was bandied more for its value to shock (if not shock then certainly to astonish) because of its supposedly inappropriate nature. Still there was an aspect of truth to what he uttered (a small, tiny aspect to be sure – but an aspect none-the-less).

'There's grotesqueness to an R. Crumb cartoon, as well,' he said. 'But there's also a wittiness and humour that one could call "charm".'

'If one wanted to misuse the word. You're the linguist…'

'Well, there's a sense of the word that means "to give delight" or "to arouse admiration"…'

'Aren't you the same person who argues that language needs to be understood in the context of the situation? Or have I miss-quoted you?'

'One also has the right to have one's own vocabulary…'

'Not if one wishes to be understood by others...'

'If you simply view Hogarth as grotesque you're missing the point...'

'You don't call babies being abused grotesque then?'

'Sure, when you analyse what you see, you might call it grotesque, but when you look at the whole picture what stands out is the wittiness. You might call a Tom and Jerry cartoon grotesque when the mouse hits the cat over the head with a giant sledgehammer but the idea is so absurd that you forget the violence and focus instead on the humour. Hogarth is like that...'

'Except Hogarth did his drawings to push a political point. People were killing themselves and abusing their children because of Demon Gin. Tom and Jerry were designed to make children laugh – though, personally, I don't see anything funny about animal violence ....(this last bit was said as more of a mutter since she really didn't want to get onto the subject of cartoon cruelty with him just now as it would take up the rest of the day debating issues that they had been round and round and round before ad nauseum).

'Hogarth was first and foremost a satirist – similar to Jonathan Swift. You can call Swift's Gulliver's Travels grotesque too if you want…'

'You're right, I wouldn't hang his book in my kitchen…'

He could tell from her face, from the wrinkling of her brow, the drawing of her lips in a serpentine motion, the narrowing of her eyes into slits that appeared to him like armour worn by errant knights getting ready to launch themselves, however unwillingly, into deep and deadly battle, that, perhaps he should ease up on her a bit.

'I promised you a coffee connection, didn't I?'

'That you did.'

'Coffee and gin. They both had a strong connection with Holland. One directly, the other indirectly. But both those commodities came to represent the duality of the new economic order – coffee was the stuff that would lubricate the wheels of commerce; gin was the stuff that would mask the pain and suffering the new economic order revealed. Think about it. A generation before, nobody had heard of gin and few people in England had ever tasted coffee. Within a few decades of the Dutch invasion, coffee houses were everyplace and gin dens had become so ubiquitous that Hogarth was driven to use them as his metaphor of consummate evil...'

'And you're blaming all this on William of Orange, are you?'

'In a manner of speaking. But I wouldn't say "blame" was the operative word here. What do you know about gin, by the way?'

'I know I don't like it. I do know it came from Holland, originally...'

'Like a lot of things we now think are bad for us, gin was invented by a doctor as a tonic for treating kidney disease and gout...'

'I thought alcohol was bad for the kidneys,' she said.

'It wasn't alcohol that was seen as the therapeutic agent; it was the juniper berry that was brewed into the drink. Dutch gin, known as jenever, became exceedingly popular almost overnight. It was easy to distil and cheap to make. And when William of Orange came to the British throne, barrels of the stuff came with him. Gin became popular in England after the government allowed unlicensed gin production and at the same time imposed a prohibitive duty on all imported spirits…'

'I don't understand,' she said. 'What possibly could have been the incentive for unleashing that terrible plague? You know what gin was called back then? "Mother's Ruin!" And that's exactly what it was!'

He arched his eyebrow – the left one, not the right. The left one was reserved for when he questioned her judgment. The right one was arched when he questioned his own.

'"Mother's Ruin" was poverty,' he said. 'Nobody spoke of "Mother's Ruin" when gin became popular amongst the middle classes.' And without waiting for her to respond, he continued, 'But as to why the government unleashed this plague, they did it for the same reason that any government unleashes plagues – it made for good business. Gin could be distilled from poor-quality grain that was unfit for brewing beer. So the government encouraged the gin trade to help prop up grain prices, which, at the time, were very low indeed. So low, in fact, that it was causing a depression in the farming industry.'

'But there was another reason...' she said. 'Pacification of the lumpen mobs...'

'That was one side of the equation. But on the other side was the wheels of commerce – and you don't keep them turning with a sozzled workforce.'

'So that's where coffee comes in, does it? But how were the Dutch involved? Coffee was already in England by then...'

'It might have been here but it was hardly known. Coffee was popularised through the network of cafes and coffeehouses relating back to the development of the financial markets that were being perfected by the Dutch…'

She looked slightly disappointed. 'That's pretty vague stuff,' she said. 'I thought you promised me a coffee connection with Seven Dials. You've gone an awful long way just to leave me with such a tenuous supposition….'

'Who said I was finished?' he told her brightly.

'Oh, God!' she muttered aloud and closed her pretty eyes.

'Hogarth, St. Giles …' He waved his hand in the direction of Bloomsbury and the steeple of St George. 'We're in the heart of Gin Lane right here, right now. Just a few decades after Neale's great urban development, the area quickly went down hill and soon became one of the worst slums in Europe. Here where we're standing was one pole in the continuum from drunkenness and despair to vigor and hopefulness. And Hogarth had a foot in both camps…'

'How so?'

'Through his father – a failed academic writer who ended up in debtor's prison and whose dream was to start…' His voice faded out as he tried to gaze into the distance through the London slime.

'…to start?' she prodded.

'To start a coffeehouse. For speakers of Latin…'

VI

So there he was, standing outside the Monmouth Coffee Company, reliving in his mind's eye that afternoon with Daisy when they had walked around the Seven Dials monument, round and round and round again, while he recited to her the convoluted history of things that popped into his head – much of which, but not all, as was recorded above. (For example, not included were things such as what he thought about the wad of gum that had stuck to the bottom of his shoe on the fourth or fifth turn.)

Now it was now. That is to say, he was in the present moment rather than in the past – where the chapter above was set. Actually, the chapter above was also in the present. It's simply that the present it related was looking back whereas this present moment, the one he was in now, was neither looking back nor forward.

Which is why he stood there, motionless.

So while Solomon is standing there, in front of the Monmouth, very obediently, neither in the past nor the future, (in what physics terms 'a state of stasis'), let us switch briefly to a moment when he and his partner, Daisy, had met at this café before.

Daisy took her coffee seriously. That's why she loved the Monmouth. Besides, it was a very woman orientated cafe – no macho baristas here, just female java guides that coffee connoisseurs (like Daisy) made into prophets for their guerrilla coffee cults. But Solomon found them a bit pretentious. It seemed to him that a certain insidious wine snobbery, which he detested from a linguistic point of view if for nothing else, was being aped. The idea of trying to mirror the Byzantine, infomercial-like prattle for wine – which had been inbuilt over the years as a way of giving value to something where nothing existed before except fermented grapes – seemed to him even more absurd for something like coffee. Wine came in a bottle and what you saw is what you got. But a sack of coffee beans was simply that – a sack of beans for making coffee. The final result – what you drank from your cup – was dependent on a series of events that included roasting, grinding and brewing, all of which added to (or subtracted from) the flavour.

'Sure,' Daisy would say accusingly, when they had one of their periodic discussions (or spats, depending on how thin-skinned they were that particular moment), 'you just use coffee the way a junkie uses speed. You're not looking for taste, just effect. And don't try to deny it!'

'I like my coffee to taste good,' he said as if to defend himself yet again from the charge of culinary barbarism. 'But what does this mean...?'

They were sitting in one of the very uncomfortable booths at the Monmouth – uncomfortable from Solomon's point of view, Daisy thought they were cosy. Solomon had picked up a coffee menu and was reading from one of the detailed descriptions of the Monmouth's specialty roasts – a Rwandan: '"Sweet blackberry notes, floral aroma and syrupy body..." What does that bloody mean?'

'It means what it says. Some people have more sensitive palates than others. But I wouldn't expect you to know anything about that...'

'I have a sensitive palate,' he shot back. 'I can tell the difference between sweet, sour, hot and mild. But "notes of sweet blackberries"? If I wanted blackberries in my coffee, I'd buy them fresh and stir them in. The thought, however, is slightly repulsive. I don't even like blackberries in my cereal.'

'Then you wouldn't want to order that particular variety, would you?'

'Well how about this one.' He pointed to the description of a medium roast Ethiopian – "Bergamot and lemon flavours with light body and bright acidity." He looked at her questioningly. 'What's "Bergamot"?'

'It's the essence from the rind of a dwarf Sevillian orange.'

'You're joking.'

She shook her head.

Sometimes he was amazed at her knowledge of the most obscure esoterica. Sometimes she was amazed at his.

He looked back at the menu. 'What's "bright acidity" then? I know what acidity is. My stomach does anyway, especially in the middle of the night. But "bright acidity"? Is that the opposite of "dark alkali"?'

"Look," she said, squinting her eyes in a manner he knew all too well, "these people are attempting to give language to subtleties of taste. That's not easy – especially as most tastes are acquired. So they're trying to relate it to flavours that people know – aromas and resonances, rather than dominant essence.'

He arched his left eyebrow (she knew his signals well). 'Bergamot?'

'It's distinctive.' Her squint relaxed and in its place the look of a tired teacher who had come to the end of her tether so many painful years ago. (God knows she tried.)

'But you're a food clod anyway so it's all lost on you…'

He shrugged. He'd been called worse. It was water off the back of a dwarf Sevillian orange, as far as he was concerned.

It wasn't only the coffee tasting ritual that made him uneasy, it was also the long and laboured descriptions of where each individual coffee bean came from, including background on the individual farmer who owned the estates that, supposedly, someone from the Monmouth had visited.

'"This month we will be visiting Guatemala to see Finca San Francisco and Finca Las Nubes, please see upcoming description lists for more information about this trip,"' he read aloud. Then, turning his gaze to his obdurate partner, he said, 'I wonder if it doubles as a holiday?'

'They're serious about their coffee,' she said. 'Would you be so facetious if it were tea?'

'I don't drink tea,' he replied. Then, looking back down at the menu, he continued reading aloud, '"La Fany is a family-owned and operated farm in the Santa Ana region. Rafael and Luis have been running the farm for the last ten years, and are the fifth generation of their family to be producing coffee. The farm started producing coffee in 1870, and is planted with the Bourbon and Pacamara varieties. Rafael has a large nursery where he cultivates his own plant stock and produces flowers for export. We visited La Fany for the first time in May 2006, and were impressed with the attention and care Rafael has for the agronomy and development of the farm. Rafael is currently experimenting with a worm farm, which produces worm stock to decompose organic matter and feed nutrients back into the soil.'"

He looked back at her again. She looked at him. There was a moment of silence.

'Don't you find that a bit...'

'A bit what?'

'...a bit much?'

'Not really.'

'Does it help us to know that Rafael is currently experimenting with a worm farm?'

'Help us do what?'

'Help us select a coffee that we'd like to bring home with us.'

'Maybe not. But what's your problem?'

'Too much irrelevant information.'

She laughed (despite her other inclination, which was either to cry or to shout.) 'You're one to talk!'

He looked somewhat confused. 'Why do you say that?'

(The reader is now referred back to the last chapter.)

(Are you done? If so we'll continue...)

'I say that because you're one to talk,' she replied.

He thought to himself that, perhaps, it was just one of her days. Then he continued reading, "'GUATEMALA. Finca Las Nubes. Chiquimula Region. Don Fabio Soliss. Lemon cream flavours with medium acidity and body. Don Fabio Solis and Dona Sonia have been growing coffee at Las Nubes since the late 1980s. The farm is located in the mountainous area of Esquipulas at approximately 1500m. This is high altitude for growing coffee, and because of the stable climate that the altitude gives, the coffee develops and matures slowly – giving a clean and sweet cup with citrus notes."'

He looked back at her again. She looked at him.

'Any problems?' she said.

'Actually, that one sounds pretty good. Except I'm not sure what lemon cream in my coffee would taste like.'

'No worse than the mouse droppings I found in your cupboard the other day, I suspect…'

'Yes. Well, I think I'll order that one…' And then he said, 'Do you think they'd hold the lemon cream, if I asked?'

VII

Now it's now again. Solomon walks into the Monmouth Coffee Company with the visions of his past experience still fresh in his head. As we can probably ferret from the brief episode above, he was not exactly smitten with the place. But Daisy was. And he was (sometimes) smitten with Daisy. So there was part of him that found the Monmouth attractive – the same part of him that found Daisy attractive, and part of him that found it annoying – the same part of him that found Daisy annoying.

What he found curious, however, is why Daisy had set his meeting with the mysterious Egyptian here of all places as there were only a few (uncomfortable) booths crunched together in the tiny back room which provided drinking space for, at most, a half dozen people.

He was mulling this over in his mind, along with thoughts of fisherman's stew with tomatoes, garlic and onions (somehow, for reasons unknown, that is what popped into his head along with the spatial query – why? Heaven knows. Or perhaps even Heaven doesn't), feeling rather grumpy (the effects of the wondrous caffeine high from earlier in the morning having worn off) when, after a moment of adjusting his eyes to the steamy darkness of the shop (which seemed to mirror London's perpetual gloom) he saw an amazing apparition.

Two amazing apparitions in one day was something of a record for Solomon. In fact, two amazing apparitions in one year or even one decade, was, in his life at least, not to be sneezed at.

This amazing apparition, however, was different from the earlier one as it was in female form. And why was it 'amazing'? It was amazing because of the reaction it evoked in him.

She was ethereal, not wholly of this world, he thought. As he gazed at her, his nostrils picked up the scent of cardamom and lemon with a bright hint of ginger. The fragrance of wild berries filled his head as he watched her delicate hands caressing the ebony handle of the espresso apparatus…

There was a sense of java all about her, from her colouring – a deep roasted mocha – to her clothes – a café au lait blouse (that accentuated the fine lines of her torso) and her silky apron, a rich café noir. Her body was panther-like: sleek, lithe and feminine. He felt an energy from across the counter, like the insistent throb of a jiggling percolator (similar to the one his mother used to make bitter black stuff when he was a child).

Perhaps she saw his mouth agape, his eyes akimbo.

'You need coffee,' she whispered. Sweetly. He didn't take sugar in his cup but he'd have gladly (madly) stirred in her charming grin.

He blinked and suddenly she disappeared behind a hiss of steam from the wild and woolly espresso maker.

'Can I take your order?'

The voice was pleasant enough, but quite

impersonal. She looked at him questioningly – as if waiting for yet another customer to make up their mind so she could get on with her work.

He glanced over at the espresso machine. The Coffee Goddess was no longer there.

'Sir?'

It was like a cartoon balloon going 'pop!' For a moment he had been soaring with angels; now he was back on earth.

She was a rather nice looking woman, the one who stood before him on the opposite side of the counter. Chinese, most likely. Dressed in ordinary street clothes rather than a uniform. She might have even been interesting in her own way. But it wasn't the same.

'I'll have a macchiato,' he said, finally, after a few moments of dumbish silence with the woman on the other side of the counter looking at him expectantly and wondering how long she was going to wait for him to respond and whether, perhaps, this customer had wandered into the wrong shop and was too embarrassed to admit that he only drank Coca Cola for breakfast which is something that had happened once before and the man that time didn't speak a word of English (except to say 'Coca Cola') which, at first, she thought was the way people said 'hello' in Azerbaijan.

So the woman behind the counter was quite relieved when Solomon said, 'I'll have a macchiato' even though she had trouble remembering how to make it as there were few people who came into the Monmouth asking for coffee drinks in Italian.

'Wouldn't you like to try one of our estate blends this morning?' she asked, hopefully.

'No,' he replied. 'Just a double shot of espresso with a smidgen of warm milk.'

Oh, yes, she recalled. That was it. She had once worked briefly at a hard-core American coffee house in Seattle and felt dreadfully intimidated by the macho barista culture with their esoteric rituals that took centuries of differing coffee traditions – Italian, French, German, Spanish, Brazilian – and ground them all into one. In Seattle espresso was king and queen and everything in between: the stronger, the darker, the better. No chance to taste the subtlety of true coffee flavours, she thought. Not like here in the Monmouth.

She brewed him a double shot, decanted it into a small enamel cup and then, twisting in a thin spiral of foamy milk that looked like the corkscrew tail of a baby pig, placed it on the counter before him as if providing an offering to a minor god.

He took a little taste and then nodded his head in satisfaction. 'That's nice,' he said, with some surprise and not a little admiration. He had sized her up as one of those reluctant drink jockeys who would never find the magic of finessing a decent cup because their heart wasn't well and truly in it. 'Quite nice, indeed,' he said, feeling a pleasant, radiant energy rush through him.

She smiled, for she loved to please her customers. It was a golden virtue she had been raised with – one that was very, very, very un-English but was endearing to her most loyal clientele and made her feel that some basic Zen circuit had been completed from server to served to server again. The English were locked in a Feudal mentality regarding service, she had noticed. So to serve became a designation of class – having undertones of servility – rather than a product of cultural pride, grace and respect.

'You made it just right,' he said. 'Some people put in too much milk. But this is perfect. Exactly the way a macchiato should be. "Macchiato" means "a mark", you see. In Italy people would often have their espresso cut with a trace of milk to moderate the bitterness. So to distinguish the cups on the tray – as one dollop of milk didn't do much to change the coffee colour – the barista would mark the milky ones with a thin trail of foam on top – just as you did.'

'I'm glad you appreciate it,' she replied. 'And thank you for the charming story about the origin of macchiato. I'll write it up in my journal so as not to forget and next time someone wanders in to order one – which happens once every five or six years – then I will relate this story back to them and they will be very impressed with my esoteric knowledge, just as I am impressed with yours.'

If it had been Daisy saying that, Solomon would have shrugged it off as facetiousness. But this woman seemed so sincere that he took it as a straightforward statement of honest feeling couched in an arcane phraseology brimming with over-politeness like too much foam from a frothy cappuccino.

'I'm glad you appreciated my story as much as I appreciated your macchiato,' he said.

'They're hard to compare,' she replied.

'Stories and coffee?'

'Something you say and something you do.'

'Can't saying be doing too?' he asked

She thought about that a moment and then said, 'Perhaps…' Which probably was a good way of nipping the conversation in the bud before it went totally out of control like quicksand where once you stick in your toe it drags you down deep into its murky depths.

'Whatever. But tell me, have you seen a man wearing a tarboosh?'

'A what?'

'You probably know it as a fez – one of those conical hats with a tassel men used to wear in the Ottoman Empire?'

What an extraordinary question to ask her, she thought. Why would a Ottoman come into the Monmouth at that hour? And the man who asked her – he did look a bit peculiar. A bit wild-eyed, she thought. Then, again, he wasn't the only unusual person to have come into the Monmouth that day. And she made a mental note to check her horoscope.

'A fez, you say?'

'Yes, a fez. A tarboosh, actually…'

'What colour?'

'Red. All fez are red. Otherwise they wouldn't be a fez.'

'What would they be if they were blue?' she asked. She shouldn't have but his cock-sure attitude was starting to annoy her.

'They'd be something else. All fez are red.'

'Couldn't one call it a "blue fez"?'

'One could but then one would be using the term "fez" improperly. Redness is built into the concept. The tassel can be blue, however…'

'So it couldn't be blue and be a fez?'

'No,' he shook his head. 'Certainly not.'

'Nor green, nor yellow?'

He shook his head again.

'In that case, no one with a fez has been in today.'

'No one?'

'No one. Unless that fellow sitting there took his off before he came in…' And she pointed to a rather large presence squeezed into a booth less than twenty feet from where they were standing.

VIII

He was a corpulent man with a plasticine face set off on the bottom by pendulous jowls and above by bushy eyebrows that had more hair than his polished head which seemed to pulsate under the ceiling light as if it were an orb used by a gypsy fortune teller. His jacket was drawn open, haphazardly, displaying his waistcoat that was buttoned all the way up to his chin. There was a white rosebud in his jacket lapel (sadly wilted) and, just below, a neatly folded handkerchief peeked out of his pocket like a mischievous rabbit misplaced by an errant magician. But the man who sat alone in the back room was not wearing a fez – red, blue or purple.

Their eyes had connected without introduction, as if to size each other up and to confirm, each in their own way, that the fat man, on one hand, and Solomon, on the other, was, indeed, the person they were to meet in this most unusual manner.

From Solomon's point of view, there seemed to be little doubt that this was his intended contact. He looked foreign and exotic and could well have been Egyptian and, furthermore, there was no one else who had crushed themselves into the abysmally narrow booths in the miniature back room that was just the right size for leprechauns and elves but not for full-bodied humans. The only problem was that the gentleman seated so uncomfortably there was wearing neither a fez nor a tarboosh. He was, as described above, glisteningly bareheaded.

As Solomon walked the several feet to the backroom, precariously balancing his macchiato cup, the (possibly) Egyptian man, made a motion with his head that could either have been a sign of recognition or of extreme discomfort − or both. And as he neared this person who was so obviously the one he had come to meet, it suddenly occurred to him that he hadn't a name except 'the Egyptian man wearing a fez' and this man was fezless. So what to say? Should he simply introduce himself first? And if he did and, by some strange circumstance, this wasn't the person he had been set up to meet (as he wasn't wearing his fez as per instructions) then a series of unwanted events could follow, such as the police being called and him being dragged off to jail for some vague sort of unwanted solicitation (this being England, after all).

This potential problem, however, was solved by the fat man, himself, who tried to stand, and, failing that, tried to smile, and, failing that, said, in a very deep and rather distinguished voice (depending on one's definition of 'distinguished'), 'I would rise to greet you, dear boy, but it appears that I am stuck...'

'Don't bother,' said Solomon, squeezing onto the wooden bench across from him. 'My friend Daisy was quite insistent I meet you here today, though she didn't give me much of an indication about what you wanted...'

The corpulent man narrowed his eyes and Solomon thought of a nature documentary he had seen not so long ago where a tiger narrowed its eyes like that just before it pounced on an innocent zebra. 'What did she tell you precisely?' asked the Egyptian.

'Precisely nothing,' Solomon replied. 'Except that I was supposed to meet a man wearing a fez at the Monmouth this morning.' Solomon lifted his gaze to the man's polished dome and raised an eyebrow.

The Egyptian sans fez pulled out his handkerchief by its rabbit-like ears and mopped his brow. 'It's rather hot in here, don't you think, Mr. Bundy?'

In fact, Solomon thought just the opposite – that it was rather chilly. But it was clear that Daisy had told the Egyptian more than she told him as the Egyptian knew his name already and he only knew the corpulent man across from him as 'the Egyptian'.

As if sensing this disparity, the Egyptian went on, 'Allow me to introduce myself. My name is Asar Mafhouz....' And reaching into a small pocket of his waistcoat – an action that resulted in a certain amount of huffing and puffing as if that very small and limited manipulation was a struggle in itself – he pulled out a business card and handed it across the narrow wooden table to Solomon, while with his other hand he mopped his brow again.

The card read: 'Asar Mafhouz, antiquarian. Dealer in fine books, jewels and collectables.' There followed two contact numbers – one in London and one in Alexandria.

Solomon stuck the card into his shirt pocket. He wished he could reciprocate with a card of his own but, to Daisy's dismay, he never got around to ordering them from the digital print operation she had methodically researched for him (sending him an initial email giving full instructions and then three follow-up reminders).

'What is it you collect?' asked Solomon.

'Personally very little, Mr. Bundy, except headaches and heartaches – but that's the human condition, isn't it?'

'It's just that your card...'

'My card?'

'The one you gave me – it said "collectables" and I wondered...'

'What I collect, Mr Bundy? Nothing for myself; only for others. I am a procurer, you see. Someone who exists to fulfil other people's fantasies.'

IX

How very strange. How very strange and curious, he thought later as he was walking back to Gower Street by way of the British Museum where he had arranged to meet Daisy for lunch. He really hadn't known what to make of him – this man whose card read: 'Asar Mafhouz, antiquarian. Dealer in fine books, jewels and collectables.' Solomon had met many antiquarian dealers in his line of work, but none quite like the Egyptian. Mostly they were exceedingly boring people who had carved out a little niche for themselves – like the elderly chap in the closet-like shop just down the road from him who specialised in Etruscan pots (which had become his whole being and essence). This little man knew more about Etruscan pottery than anyone else in the world. People came from very far off places just to consult with him about something they thought might be anciently

Italian. He would take one look and date it with far more accuracy than the boys at the lab could do with all their high-tech paraphernalia. But there was no mystery about him. He was an Etruscan pot, pure and simple. He even said so himself. ('You know that book entitled, I am a Camera? Well, I am a pot.' And he would shape his creaky bones into a spout and a handle.)

This man, this Egyptian, was not simple at all. He was interested in 'collectables' – but what? He wasn't an Egyptologist – not one of those dry and dusty 'tomb raiders' hawking another finely crafted forgery (or not so fine) with a story that always entailed a Pharaoh's curse and a trail of mysterious deaths (just for good measure). No, this man wasn't part of the 'Cairo Mob' (as he called them); he was from Alexandria – a wondrous city that owed as much to Greece and Rome as to the Ottomans. Once the crossroads of the world, it was the place, more than even Constantinople ('had been', he actually said, emphasising that it was once in the past and, sadly, no more), where East and West met on equal terms and shared or bought or sold all that was best in their various cultures.

So what was it about him that Solomon found so intriguing? And why had he accepted the Egyptian's offered commission? Perhaps it was the essence of the bean, he thought. For the Egyptian gentleman, like Daisy, was obsessed with the story of coffee. In fact, as Solomon discovered, that was their connection. Daisy had come across some curious coins without denomination, shown to her by a colleague from the university archaeological department who had found them on a recent dig in central London where a lovely old building had been torn down to make way for an ugly new one and, as usual, the department sent out a team to sift through the debris (two days, no more) and found bits and pieces of the 17th and 18th centuries including these strange coins which Daisy was shown and she, in turn, contacted the

Egyptian who, she was told, was an expert in coffee tokens, and he then confirmed what she had suspected.

'But not 17th century, sweet lady,' he said. '18th, I would think...'

'Why is that?' she asked, inspecting the coin under the high magnification scope again. 'The Turk's Head used tokens as early as 1680...'

'The image is based on Sultaness Aseki – a lithograph by Bernard Picart in 1721.'

She told Solomon this when they met for lunch at the rotunda of the British Museum and she said it between bites of her smoked salmon sandwich.

'Coffee tokens...?' The expression on his face completed the sentence.

'They had an exhibit here of tradesmen's tokens a while back,' she said. 'I think I told you about it...'

Maybe she had. But she also told him about exhibitions of chipped ceramic vases.

'The government was struggling with a shortage of metal – especially copper – in the sixteen and seventeen hundreds. At the same time there was an amazing growth in small shops and business...'

He nodded. London was an open city back then, drawing merchant adventurers and rag-tag itinerants to this vortex of new and untapped finance. Fortunes were being gained in a single day (and lost in a single evening). And the epicentre of this moneyed tempest was the coffeehouse.

'The idea of people using their own currency of exchange wasn't new,' he said. 'But the government never welcomed the competition. The right to control money and script was essential to their authority...'

'Except there wasn't much they could do about it,' she said. 'Especially in the area of small coinage. If you didn't have change, you still had to provide your client with something. Tradesmen's tokens were a logical development. The government tried to ban them – but it was a half-hearted attempt. The tradesmen were simply fulfilling a need and the value of the tokens was usually small – a penny at best. But eighteenth century London was flooded with them.'

'What did they use for their coins if metal was in such short supply?' he asked.

'Whatever was available. The government was obliged to use pure metal of worth; traders were not. They even used leather sometimes. These tokens, after all, only had value at the place that issued it...'

'So it became something like a loyalty card...'

'Something like that. It also was a form of advertising. I guess you could say it was the beginnings of jingles and slogans...'

'What kind of slogan could you fit on a coin?' he said.

'You'd be surprised. But as most people couldn't read, it didn't much matter. What mattered was the image...'

'So the logo had to be easily recognisable...'

'And they had to project very simple, easy to understand ideas.'

'That's the beginning of the commodity culture, isn't it?' he said. 'Selling reality through fantasy images. It doesn't have to be very sophisticated. The earliest radio transmissions, crackly and tinny as they were, had a powerful affect on the imagination. Probably even more than today's computer generated reality that leaves nothing for the mind's eye to shape and mould…'

'We're getting down to the nitty-gritty basics, aren't we?'

She smiled at him. He smiled at her. They were having fun. And herein we discover the secret of their most curious relationship. Daisy and Solomon truly enjoyed bandying about ideas that most other people would find dreadfully dull and tedious. But look at them, dear reader. See them sitting together at that charming café set in the beautiful rotunda of one of the most remarkable architectural settings in the (occasionally) fair city of London. Are they appreciative of this splendid view passed down to them by some of the world's most talented and masterful (though, sadly, unknown) builders? Or are they so wrapped up in pursuing a minor bit of arcane trivia that all these wondrous delights of civilisations past are lost on them?

Actually, not.

For both Solomon and Daisy the British Museum was the epicentre of their existence – both separate and together. Solomon had taken rooms on Gower Street so the museum and the library were within easy reach. Daisy used it as an adjunct for her work at the Archaeological Institute. But beyond the utilitarian function this place served, they both loved it for other, more intangible things it could provide; this place was also their spiritual home as well as the font for their unquenchable scholarly cravings.

It was to Hans Sloane, a naturalist and physician from Ulster, that the world – at least the world Solomon believed in – owed an enormous debt. He had found the good chap's picture in a curio shop, had it framed and hung it in his kitchen right next to the Hogarth and when Daisy had questioned him about his very curious taste in art (or artistic positioning), he replied that Sir Hans Sloane was a hero to him of sorts and thus should have pride of place in his rather cramped quarters – and where better to put him than by the drinks table?

'Why the drinks table?'

'Because he discovered chocolate…'

'Surely not. Chocolate was discovered by the Aztecs!'

'Yes, but Sloane discovered drinkable chocolate. Made it into a powder and mixed it with sugar and milk. Before that it was a bitter brew. Made most people nauseous.'

'When are we talking about?'

'This was in the 1680s, 1690s – about the time coffee was starting to emerge into the city's consciousness.'

'And that's the same Sloane who started the British Museum?' she asked him, pointing to the etching of the avuncular gentleman, his wig flowing in a thick, curly stream down the front of his knitted jacket. She felt drawn to his eyes – his large, sleepy eyes. The eyes of a dreamer, she thought. An aspergian dreamer…

'He was one of those *wunderkammer* people – you know…'

'Yes. The Cabinet of Curiosity. I loved the notion. When I first heard the term as a child I imagined a wonderful Alice-in-Wonderland world in a box, until someone told me that 'cabinet' was meant in the French sense of the word – like an office – and then the whole thing went "poof!"' She had stopped momentarily and looked at him with eyes also of a dreamer and said, 'Why can't children be left to their fantasies?'

He knew what she meant, for, he too had been one of those children with a rich and wonderful fantasy life who had wished really to have been Peter Pan and never to have grown up (if he ever had).

'There were tons of them in the 17th century, all throughout Europe. Collectors would devise these rooms with their own special vision – they were incredibly eclectic – exotic plants and animals, rocks, gems, ethnographic artefacts, the strange and the bizarre. And yet they all had a unity because it was one person's collection, one curator who was drawn to organise all these diverse, eccentric objects into a theatrical display of the absurd and the grotesque, creating their very own notion of an interconnected universe.'

'So who was he, this Sloane...' She motioned to the etching affixed to a hook on Solomon's wall. 'Who was this man who gave his name to air-headed Sloanies and a square that I do my best to avoid?'

'A physician to the stars. An intelligent man, but no great thinker. He had an encyclopaedic mind and a thirst for knowledge and he gave over his collections and his home to the state, which eventually became the British Museum. It's not much in the scheme of things, I guess, but there's something magical about planting a seed like that and then here we are over two hundred years later…'

And there they were, over two hundred years later, sitting in the splendid rotunda of a place that Hans Sloan could hardly, in his most dreamy of dreams, ever have imagined.

X

'So what did the Egyptian want you to do?' she asked.

'You mean you don't know?' To say he was flabbergasted is a bit off the mark. He was well acquainted with Daisy's ways, after all. 'I thought you spoke with him. It was you who set this up…'

'And it was you who needed work…'

'Well, how do you know he didn't offer me something illegal?'

'Like what?'

'Like getting involved in a swindle…'

'A swindle?'

'Or a heist…'

'A heist?' She looked at him and laughed. Trying to picture Solomon as part of a gang of crooks was difficult – unless the gang was kin to the Lavender Hill Mob.

'What's so funny?' He found her laughter annoying. Especially when it was directed at him. But when she laughed, her face took on a lovely glow, so he couldn't be annoyed at her long.

'Nothing.' She straightened her lips but it was too much. The muscles in her face just couldn't hold the surge of frivolity that pushed from inside her abdomen, up her throat and into her mouth, and then gushed forth as a stream of tittering giggles.

That annoyed him even more – lovely glow or not. It was like a veiled attack on his deepest, most adolescent fears from playground notions of manhood. And it made him puff up his chest. 'You don't think I could make a good crook?'

She really was trying to hold back her giggles but it just didn't work. Especially seeing him like that, all in a blather, like a clucking rooster flapping its feathers. But Daisy knew she was somehow stepping over an invisible line that exists between all couples whether they know it or not. So she took his hand in hers and said, in the most charming voice she could muster, 'You're sweet...'

It was absolutely, positively and most certainly the wrong thing to utter. What he wanted her to say, though he would never admit it even if he were made to stand on burning embers (well, maybe not burning embers – squishy peas, perhaps) – what he wanted her to say was, 'I know you're very brave and, like Clark Kent and Superman, if it came right down to it, I'm certain you would thrust off your spectacles, put on your cape and save the human race from annihilation and me from certain death.' And she would have had to say it in those precise words. Anything else just wouldn't have been good enough.

He pulled back his hand and looked at her in a sulk.

'I'm sorry,' she said.

'There's no apology necessary,' he replied between his teeth.

She sighed and then reached down to her motley brown sack (the kind adventurers take with them into the jungles) and pulled out an envelope. 'Look,' she said, smiling again. It was a different sort of smile this time directed toward the little boy in him. 'I have something for you…'

'For me?' he said, glancing at the parcel-like envelope.

She nodded.

'Can I open it?'

She nodded again.

He opened the little packet, gently pulling up the corners with a practiced touch – a technique he acquired from years of dealing with precious documents that needed special care lest they turn back into dust. In fact he even carried with him a pair of white cotton gloves just in case he needed them.

Peering inside the packet through the opening he had methodically created, he saw a small object which he carefully eased into his open hand.

It was a coin, very old from its appearance, quite discoloured and rough around the edges.

'For me?' he asked again, glancing back at her.

'For you to look at,' she replied. 'Actually, I have to return it to the department…'

He inspected the little coin. On the face, he could make out the image of a woman; on the obverse, very faintly, the letters, 'M-O-R-A-T'.

'Is this the coffee token you showed the Egyptian?' he asked.

'Yes.'

Turning the coin over in his hand, he examined both sides again. 'How could he tell this was the image of the Sultaness – what's her name again?'

'Aseki…'

'How could he tell it was her image?' he asked.

'I don't know. But I found the Picart lithograph and it certainly has a strong similarity.'

He brought the face of the coin closer to his eye. 'It's such a sketchy outline. I can't see how anyone could make a definite connection like that..'

'Neither can I,' she said. 'And there are some other curiosities as well…'

'Such as?'

She took his hand, the one that was holding the coin-like object, and turned the token over, pointing to the lettering on the obverse.

'Morat's was a coffee house in London. Quite popular. We've found lots of tokens – pennies and half pennies ...'

'Where was it located?

'By the Royal Exchange, where a great many coffee houses were located. Morat's was one of the best known. They also sold coffee powder and berries for customers to take home and roast themselves – along with a set of instructions on how to brew it because coffee was so new back then.'

Holding this object, tiny as it was, gave him a powerful feeling of connection with something deep and dark and mysterious. He probably couldn't have described this strange sensation if asked because it was very different from others he had experienced and thus there was little to compare. Of course, working with ancient documents had often given him a visceral sense of the past – something he could taste on the tip of his tongue rather than the sensory quiescence from flat, dullish factlets one found pressed into re-printed books or in digitalised form on the Internet. But this small piece of nothing that rested awkwardly in the palm of his hand, this base metal object lost for many centuries in an urban dump and recently unearthed, had a strange, exotic energy to it.

She took a jeweller's scope from her bag and passed it to him. 'See if you can make out the writing around the periphery – on the obverse...'

He turned the coin over in his hand and inspected it through the scope. 'It's difficult to make out...' he said.

'We did a UV photo...' she said and rummaging in her bag she found some sheets of paper, which she pulled out, gingerly, and handed to him.

The size of the coin had been enlarged by 400 percent and the contrast adjusted so the writing could now easily be deciphered:

'Morat Y Great Men Did Mee Call / Where Eare I Came I Conquered All.'

He tried sifting through his rusty memory banks for 'Morat' without success. 'I'm not familiar with the name,' he confessed.

'Amurath IV. An Ottoman sultan who ruled from around 1625 to 1640. His head appears on 30 or so London coffee house tokens that used a Turk's head as a symbol…'

Solomon looked at the face of the coin again. 'But not this one…'

'That's why it's so unusual. This is the head of a sultaness…'

Brushing his finger lightly over the face, he said, 'A sultaness without a veil…'

'England's fascination with the Turk – sultans and sultanesses – was insatiable back then. So coffee houses used their imagery to good effect. There was even a coffee house called "The Sultiness", in fact…'

'So maybe the Morat token was adapted to tempt men with both power and sex,' he suggested. 'I suspect that worked even back then...'

'The only problem is...' Her voice trailed off.

'Is what?' He didn't like lingering thoughts. They were like half-baked buns – alluring while still in the oven but you didn't know what they'd taste like till you ate them.

'If the Egyptian is right, then the image is based on an 18th century lithograph...'

He shrugged. 'Coffee shops still used tokens in the 18th century, didn't they?'

'A few. But minting coins for small change was no longer tolerated by then...'

'This one doesn't have a denomination,' he reminded her. 'Maybe it was simply used as an advertisement...'

'Maybe. But there's still a big problem placing it in the 18th century...'

'Problems are the staff of life – even more than bread,' he reminded her.

'Morat's Coffee House was destroyed in the Great Fire of 1666. It was never rebuilt again...'

XI

Solomon loved the old British Library when it was housed in the Museum. He loved the structure and its aura. Just being there brought something special, something precious and revered, passed down through centuries of scholars – not academics but freelance researchers from all walks of life who cherished this place as much as he did. There was a feeling, upon entering that magnificent circular hall beneath the ornate rotunda, similar to entering a most hallowed cathedral. Except here the deities were of the mind and of the word that could well be blasphemous. Yet all who entered, be they prince or pauper, once there were equals. Seated on those green upholstered chairs, set before desks of finely polished wood arranged in concentric rows of magic circles, one communed, not with the gods, but with the human spirit at its best and most magnificent. And for moments, brief as they were, all who entered this sanctorum could, if they so wished, connect with the shimmering fairies who might whisper in their ear the secrets of the universe.

It was, for Solomon, the shrine of all things good and sacred as well as all things profane and evil. It was, in short, all things. But all things in a space that imbued them with a sense of awe and wonder.

The new British Library on Euston Road was different. It was clean and well lit, systematised and – to him, at least – soulless. Of course, it was much more efficient – as most books were now stored on site rather than repositories scattered about town. In the old days readers would request books that might end up arriving days later or, like a surprise visitor, appear mysteriously on their desk when least expected. But how long it took for a volume to arrive didn't really make all that much difference to the serious researchers who came on a daily basis. If one planned it right, there was a steady flow of books. They arrived in no particular order, so work was organised around what was available at any specific moment.

The new place seemed to take its cue from high-tech factory culture. Computer-savvy readers put in their book requests online and picked up their titles upon arrival at the collections desk (staffed by faceless clerks who, he believed, had a clause in their contract forbidding them to smile). The reading rooms had desks arranged in rows that were orderly and unbendingly rigid, as befitting the Office for the Production and Dissemination of Facts and Data. The toilets were sanitised and would have done the Hilton proud. The airport-like café was linked to the Internet by high-speed Wi-Fi.

So what was lost and what was gained in this New Age shift when that ancient, fuddy-duddy library under the vast rotunda was moved to the revitalised megalopolis by King's Cross? What was gained was speed. What was lost was magic.

Solomon had a foot in both camps. He was young enough to have built a dependency on his portable computer and old enough to have experienced the romance of the ancient library and all its spirits and its ghosts before it was laid to rest and then reborn, a literary Phoenix, in its contemporaneously digitalised form. Part of him could deal with the new place quite nicely, once he plugged himself in. Part of him, though, continued to wonder what happened to people like the delightfully winsome and white-headed woman with a twinkle in her eyes, researching a book on the history of sex (who explained to him in minute detail the ancient Roman practice of fellatio) or the gentlemanly old dosser working his way, methodically, through all the literature on Amazonian butterflies, present and past, trying to discover where they would go after the rain-forest was eventually denuded. '"They shine curiously like the stars and do cast about them sparks of the colours of the Rainbow" – a quote from Sir Theodore de Mayerne on butterfly wings in 1634,' he had told him.

They disappeared after the move and he never saw them afterwards.

He stayed around to reminisce after Daisy left to go back to her office. She was always in a hurry. He wasn't. Or tried not to be, anyway. Sometimes, of course, circumstances required him to quicken his pace. Then he would inject himself with more caffeine and let his engine rev for a while. He didn't need much sleep and could keep at a project for hours on end – as long as there was a pitcher of coffee at hand.

Below, the old reading room had been returned to the museum – in spirit (in substance it always was). He saw it as a montage of layers past and present. Each layer was stratified above the one below but the montage allowed the various pasts to be flattened and compressed into one, creating another time zone in his mind. It was the zone of free-floating memory. There, characters from the past could interact with those from the future. Those who once were could speak with those yet to be and those who now are could splice themselves together with those who are no longer. And seated in the heights of the rotunda, he watched it all take place as if he were in a private box above this theatre of the grandiose which evolved like a paramecium gaining cells, then gills, then legs from a simple cabinet of curiosities to his window on so many wonders.

'So what is it the Egyptian wanted you to do?' she had asked him.

It's strange she hadn't asked the Egyptian himself, but Daisy was Daisy and, thus, quasi-predictable. She was happy enough to have found him work – whatever it was.

'He wanted something translated...'

'Yes, I gathered that. You're a translator, aren't you? I didn't expect he would ask you to whitewash the walls of his office.'

'He wasn't wearing a hat, you know...'

'What? I'm sorry, I thought we were talking about your new translation assignment...'

'You said he would be wearing a fez. He wasn't.'

'He was when I met him.'

'He wasn't then.'

'But you found him didn't you? So why the fuss?'

'I found him because he was the only one there…'

'But you found him, didn't you?'

'I could not have found him if there were others…'

'How many fat Egyptians could have fit in there?'

'That's another thing. Why did you arrange the meeting at the Monmouth?'

'Why not?'

'It's small.'

'If it were big maybe ten fat Egyptians could have been comfortably sat and you might not have found him and then you would have had something to blame me for instead of thanking me, as I deserve, for finding you work.'

She was right, of course, and he accepted that (though he wouldn't admit it).

He had pulled out the envelope from his

jacket pocket and handed it to her. (It was, in a sense, a fair trade. She showed him hers; he showed her his.)

'What is it?' she had asked, after opening the envelope (without the obsessive care he had shown hers, it should be said), pulling out the single sheet of paper, unfolding it and smoothing it out with the side of her hand.

'It is what you see.'

'What I see appears to be the picture of an amulet. It's charming but I don't know how you'd translate it...'

'Look closer. What do you see?'

She had brought the picture closer to her eyes. 'It looks like a necklace of some sort with three kidney-shaped pendants...'

'Coffee beans – at least that's what the Egyptian said.'

'Three coffee beans constructed into some sort of amulet.' She had looked back at him. 'They're black...'

'Black gold, he said.'

'Black gold?'

'I like the idea. Sort of like green snow...'

'I've heard of black gold. It's used sometimes in jewellery. Don't know whether it exists in nature, but I can find out...' She had studied the picture and still couldn't see what his job would entail.

'Use your little scope,' he had told her. 'The beans have scratch marks – do you see them?'

'Very faintly. Could be some sort of cuneiform, I guess. But how can you translate something like that?'

It's what he had said to the Egyptian.

'I can't translate something I can't see. Don't you have a better image?'

'No, dear boy. This is what I was given.'

'By whom?'

'By my client.'

'Ask your client for a larger image then...'

'I'm sad to relate that this is the best my client has.'

Solomon was annoyed by then. He was annoyed at Daisy for setting this up. He was annoyed at being squeezed into an uncomfortable booth across from a bald headed fat man. And he was annoyed at himself for spending a good part of his morning going around loops and circles. 'It seems like a fairly ridiculous project,' he had told the Egyptian.

'Dear boy, I was afraid you'd say that.' The Egyptian had pursed his lips like someone who had eaten a quince or a sour tomato. 'Of course it would be made well worth your while…'

'To do what?'

'To do what it is you do, of course.'

'But in order to translate something you need to be able to see what it is you're to translate. That's number one. Number two, the language that the word represents must be one that I know. And number three…' He couldn't think of number three, so he just let it go at numbers two and one.

'And you accepted?' Daisy had said, when he showed her the image at lunch.

'I didn't accept and I didn't not accept.'

'That sounds to me as if you accepted.'

'I accepted to think about it.'

'And have you thunk?'

'I am thunking, I have thunk, I will continue to thunk.'

She packed up her gear. 'I've got to dash.'

'You always have to dash,' he reminded her.

She had bent over to give him a quick little kiss. 'See you this evening,' she said as she started to leave.

'Wait, you forgot something,' he called after her.

'What?' She turned back to him.

He handed her the envelope with the image the Egyptian had given him. 'See if your brilliant young technician can do something with it...'

And then she had left and there he was, alone, lost in his imagination. 'Ho, hum,' he said to himself. And looking down at the table, he noticed that Daisy had made a little bird out of her napkin. She always had restless fingers, he thought. Everything about her was restless – her mind, her feet, her hands...

He picked up the origami napkin and played with it. Pulling the tail made its wings flap. Then, for no reason (no readily explainable one, that is), he took out his pen and wrote something on each wing, launched the transformed napkin into the air and watched as it set forth on its new life, sailing over the side of the mezzanine and gliding down to great hall below.

The waiter, a thin young man with a quizzical look on his face and a tattoo of a ladybug on his forehead, came up to his table and folded his arms. 'You know, you're the third person today who did that,' he said.

'Three is an interesting number,' Solomon replied. 'It's the first odd prime. It's a triangle – the most durable of shapes. And it's the largest number written with the same amount of lines that it represents.'

'It's also the maximum number of times a joke can be repeated and still be funny,' the waiter said. 'I saw you write something on the wings. What was it?'

Solomon looked at the young man and wondered what it was like being a waiter up here – like Gabriel guarding the gates of Heaven. 'I wrote "*veni*" on one wing and "*vidi*" on the other.'

The waiter thought a moment and then said, 'Oh, well, that's all right then.'

XII

What he had really wanted to tell her about was the amazing coffee experience he had that morning when he came across the strange little kiosk on Gower Street that served the best coffee in the world (at least according to him). But talking with Daisy was sometimes like talking to the wind – conversations were likely to be blown all over the place, sometimes as far as a run-down cigar factory in the westernmost reaches of Cuba. Often, in the past, when he had something important to tell her, he would write it on a slip of paper and pin it to her rucksack so that it existed, at least, in written form because orally it was quite likely to get lost in a maelstrom of excitable electrons.

But when he went back to his rooms later that day, passing by the location where Pasqua's little coffee kiosk had been set up that morning, he found, to his extreme disappointment, it was no longer there. And asking at the neighbouring shops provided no help whatsoever. ('You want coffee? There's a Starbucks round the corner...')

Did he imagine it? If he did, it was the most amazing hallucination he had ever experienced (not that he had experienced many unless, as he sometimes suspected, life was just one humongous hallucination, itself). But then, there was the extraordinary Coffee Goddess at the Monmouth that morning – the one who had disappeared behind the veil of steam while he stood there agog. He was quite prepared to explain her away as just one of those erotic delights that cropped up occasionally in phantasmagorical form when least expected – even though she, too, seemed real enough. But he hadn't drunk her brew as he had done with Pasqua.

He checked his tongue in the mirror as he did occasionally when he wasn't feeling well. Not that he was sure what he was looking for, but sticking one's tongue out and observing it in the mirror was something that from childhood seemed to be the thing to do when diagnosing some mysterious illness that had little signs or symptoms. (He didn't carry many of his childhood phobias into the more rational world of adults – few that he recognised, anyway – but inspecting his tongue in the mirror was one. Actually, he wasn't sure what he was supposed to find out by going through this ritual except that 1. it was still there; 2. it hadn't swollen twice its size; or 3. it wasn't a deadly shade of lavender – but he did it anyway like some people do when they stick a thermometer in their mouth and then spend twenty minutes or so trying to read the thing by which time the mercury had fallen far below normal.)

Then he checked 'hallucinations' in Wikipedia on his computer:

'Studies have now shown hallucinatory experiences take place across the population as a whole. Previous studies, one as early as 1894, have reported that approximately 10% of the population experience hallucinations. A recent survey of over 13,000 people reported a much higher figure with almost 39% of people reporting hallucinatory experiences, 27% of whom reported daytime hallucinations, mostly outside the context of illness or drug use. From this survey, olfactory (smell) and gustatory (taste) hallucinations seem the most common in the general population.'

OK, so maybe he wasn't crazy. Or maybe between 27 and 39 percent of the population was just as crazy as he was.

Not that he was actually frightened about losing his sanity. He felt as grounded as one could, given the frailties of 21st century existence. In fact, these hallucinations – if, indeed, that's what they were – were intriguing as well as disquieting. He had a natural urge to find meaning in meaninglessness. (In fact, 'meaninglessness' was a concept he had trouble with. Everything, in his way of thinking, had meaning – even if you had to invent one yourself.)

The idea of hallucination also interested him from a linguistic perspective. The word, itself, took you in several directions: one was the notion of fantasy and imagination (sugar-fairies and poets); the other was darker and more sinister (nightmares and chimeras). There were the competing ideas of delirium (illness) and visions (tripping): apparition versus illusion; medical versus spiritual; hope versus despair. (What did the students in 1968 really mean when they shouted, 'All power to the imagination?' Would the slogan 'All power to the hallucination!' have had the same ring to it?)

Down through the ages, hallucinations meant different things. Hearing voices could be either dangerous (if the voices seemed to be diabolical) or illuminating (if they came from God). Dante's descent into Hell was an hallucinatory experience par excellence. The oracle at Delphi was helped along by magical mushrooms. The poets of the Haight/Ashbury found their muse in psilocybin; Van Gogh's throbbing colours and undulating lines could have been engendered by brain waves similar to the epileptic. And yet these visions all were windows of perception. Poets, writers, painters, musicians – each gained their muse in ways that others, less blessed, might view as madness.

All of which is to say, in a rather long-winded manner, that Solomon was not too perturbed about seeing visions (if that's what they were), even if he did check his tongue in the mirror and google 'hallucination' into his computer. Explorers who venture into the freezing snows of the Arctic can expect frostbite on their toes and fingers. Those who venture into the equally severe reaches of the mind, can expect something akin in their head. It's the nature of the beast, Solomon thought – when he actually thought about it.

With that he put aside his vague apprehensions (after all his visions had been exceptionally pleasant) and made ready for the evening event as requested by Daisy, his partner in delusional conundrums.

Then he looked down at the clock adhered to his trusty cup, the one with the silly, maniacal grin. 'COFFEE TIME!!!' it shouted.